CELESTE and REGINE in the RAIN FOREST

written by FRANCES GILBERT

illustrated by SARAH FRANCES

Greene Bark Press

Publisher's Cataloging-in-Publication
(Provided by Quality Books, Inc.)

Celeste and Regine in the rain forest

Gilbert, Frances.
　　Celeste and Regine in the rain forest / written by Frances Gilbert and illustrated
by Sarah Frances.
　　p.　　cm.
　　Preassigned LCCN: 97-71280
　　ISBN: 1-880851-28-8
　　SUMMARY: Two small tree frogs find their rain forest home threatened by the
arrival of two strange creatures.
　　1. Hylidae—Juvenile fiction. 2. Rain forest—Juvenile fiction.
3. Tree frogs. I. Frances, Sarah. II. Title.
PZ8.3.G553Ce 1997　　　　　　　　　　　[E]
　　　　　　　　　　　　　　　　　QBI97-40400

To the memory of Elsie Weighill
and for Little Sarah
generation to generation

Celeste and Regine spend carefree days in their rain forest home.

Up in the cackling canopy, down on the sun-speckled forest floor, and all the leafy, shady places in between, go Celeste and Regine.

. . . bothering the butterflies for 'butterfly breeze'
in the damp-smelling mornings,

. . . playing slap-the-sloth in the lazy, hazy afternoons,

. . . mocking the monkeys until 'monkey howl' rolls around the forest in the purple-gathering evenings,

Then Celeste and Regine run to Old Mama, where safely

tucked under her folds and bulges they watch the forest

breathing in,

breathing out,

as it always has,

generation to generation.

Night fills the forest gaps.

"Listen!" says Old Mama, "listen!"

. . . frog song, mellowing, resounding,

blending into the night full and vibrant,

telling the magic of the forest,

the secrets of its ancient peoples,

their healing powers,

the enchantment of its ancient worlds.

"We are the keepers of the lore," they sound,

"We know the forest's story, generation to

generation."

"Oh," cried Celeste, and "Oh," whispered Regine.

"We want to be part of it."

"One day you will," said Old Mama.

And so it went,

until one peaceful morning,

strange yellow creatures arrived screaming,

clawing the ground,

big orange insects hovered,

buzzing and snapping at the trees.

"What are they?" whimpered Celeste.

"What is happening?" sobbed Regine.

Old Mama wept,

tears rolled down her wrinkles.

She could not speak.

That night frog-song was deep and sad.

"It is the end," mourned the older frogs, ". . . the end."

"The forest is disappearing," cried Celeste.

"We must do something to stop it," said Regine.

So off they went,

up in the silent canopy,

down on the wasting forest floor

and in all the leafless, open places in between,

. . . until they found someone to tell,

who put it in a book.

So now you know the story of the rain forest, and can
help to save it for all of us to hand on, just as it always
has been,

generation to generation,

for ever.

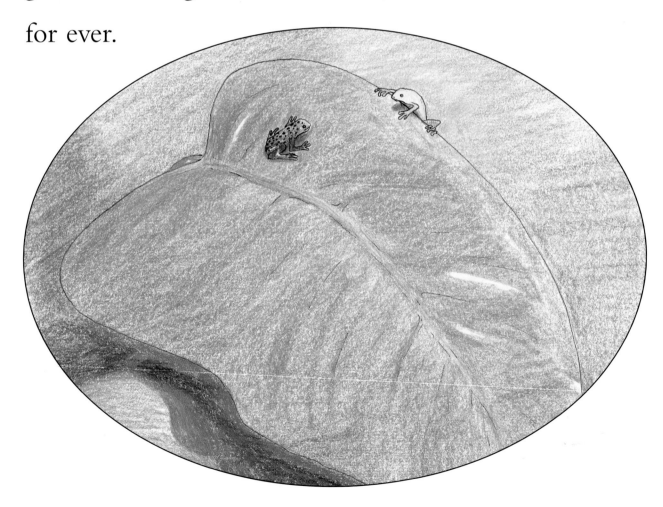